Also by Rachael Reed

Codefendant

Codefendant

Once a Cheater

Once a Cheater

Passport Bro

What Happens in Prison

Preference

Sprinkle Sprinkle

Championship Bad

Street Exodus

Street Exodus

Street Royalty

Pawns of Power

SIS

Cartel Bloodline

Get Money Girls

Skip the Games

Til Death Do Us Part

Backpage Hustle

Backpage Hustle

Backpage Hustle
By Rachael Reed
Copyright © 2024 by Rachael Reed
Check Out More Great Products and Free Giveaways
https://tbdbpublishing.com/

Chapter 1: Project Beginnings

Theresa Graham leaned against the peeling wall of her small apartment, staring out the dirty window at the projects below. The air was thick with the stench of despair and the distant wail of sirens. She'd grown up in these streets, seen every grimy corner of the hood, and learned the hard way that survival meant playing the game or getting played.

Theresa was an escort, hustling on Backpage to make ends meet. She didn't sugarcoat her life. She knew exactly what it was: a daily grind in a world that didn't give a damn about her. But she had a plan, a dream to rise above the muck and claim the life she believed she deserved. She was determined to change her fate, no matter the cost.

She flipped open her laptop, the screen flickering to life. Her Backpage profile was up, her photos and services listed for all to see. She'd cultivated an image, a brand that kept the money rolling in. "Sugar" was the name she used on the site—a name that promised sweet, unforgettable experiences. The reality was far less glamorous.

"Yo, Sugar, you got another date lined up?" called out Keisha, her best friend and roommate, from the tiny kitchen. Keisha knew the hustle too well, always covering for Theresa when things got rough.

"Yeah, got a john coming through in an hour," Theresa replied, her voice flat. "Another night, another dollar."

She closed the laptop and moved to the bathroom, looking at herself in the mirror. Her face was tired, the makeup unable to hide the weariness in her eyes. She brushed her long, dark hair, thinking about how she ended up here. She remembered the nights she'd spent on these same streets as a kid, watching her mama struggle to keep a roof over their heads.

Theresa's childhood was a blur of hardship and heartache. Her mama had worked two, sometimes three jobs, just to keep food on the table. But the projects were a harsh place, and Theresa had learned early on that if she wanted something, she had to take it. School hadn't held her interest—she'd dropped out at sixteen, hitting the streets to make money the only way she knew how.

Her first pimp had been a lowlife named Rico. He'd shown her the ropes, introduced her to Backpage, and took most of her earnings. It wasn't long before Theresa realized she was just another pawn in his game. She'd cut ties with Rico, determined to make it on her own terms. She built her reputation as Sugar, using her beauty and street smarts to attract clients and keep herself safe.

But the hustle was relentless. Every night brought new dangers, new challenges. She'd been robbed, beaten, and nearly killed more times than she cared to remember. The streets showed no mercy, and she had to stay sharp to survive.

As she finished her makeup, Theresa's phone buzzed. A text from her next client: "Be there in 20." She sighed, slipping into a tight dress that accentuated her curves. It was all part of the game—look the part, play the part, get paid.

"Yo, Keisha, I'm heading out," she called, grabbing her purse.

Keisha appeared in the doorway, concern etched on her face. "Be careful out there, girl. You know these fools ain't playin' fair."

Theresa nodded, a grim smile on her lips. "I got this. Ain't nothin' I can't handle."

She stepped out into the night, the cool air hitting her like a slap. The streets were alive with activity—drug dealers on the corners, kids playing under the flickering streetlights, and the constant hum of danger in the air. She moved with purpose, her heels clicking on the cracked pavement, her eyes scanning for any sign of trouble.

Her client was a middle-aged man with a paunch and a receding hairline. He met her in front of a rundown motel, his eyes hungry and desperate. Theresa put on her best smile, playing the role she'd perfected over the years.

"Hey there, handsome," she purred, slipping her arm through his. "Ready for a good time?"

He nodded eagerly, and they headed inside. The room was dingy, the bed covered in a threadbare blanket. Theresa went through the motions, her mind detached from the act. It was just another night, another transaction.

Afterward, she walked back to her apartment, the weight of the night heavy on her shoulders. She hated this life, but it was all she knew. The streets had shaped her, hardened her, but they hadn't broken her. Not yet.

As she climbed the stairs, her phone buzzed again. This time, it was a message from Big D. She'd heard of him—an old-school pimp with a reputation for getting things done. He wanted to meet, said he had a proposition for her. Theresa's heart quickened. This could be the opportunity she'd been waiting for, a chance to change the game in her favor.

She unlocked the door and stepped inside, her mind racing. Keisha looked up from the couch, a question in her eyes.

"Who was it?" she asked.

"Big D," Theresa replied, a smile playing at her lips. "He wants to meet. This could be it, Keisha. This could be my way out."

Keisha nodded, hope and fear mingling in her gaze. "Just be careful, T. This life ain't never what it seems."

Theresa nodded, determination steeling her resolve. She was ready to gamble it all, to risk everything for a shot at something better. The streets had taught her well, but she was ready to rewrite the rules.

As she lay in bed that night, her mind buzzing with possibilities, Theresa knew one thing for certain: she wasn't going to be another casualty of the projects. She was going to rise, no matter what it took. The game was far from over, and she was just getting started.

Chapter 2: Meeting Big D

Theresa sat in a dimly lit bar, nursing a drink and trying to unwind after another long night on Backpage. The place was filled with the usual crowd—hustlers, dealers, and girls like her looking to make a quick buck. She scanned the room, her eyes landing on a man sitting in the back, surrounded by a group of men who seemed to hang on his every word.

Derrick "Big D" Poindexter was a legend in the streets, a seasoned pimp with connections that ran deep. He was known for his power and influence, a man who could make or break you with a single word. Tonight, he was dressed in a sharp suit, his eyes sharp as they scanned the room, taking in everything and everyone.

Theresa had heard about Big D, but she'd never crossed paths with him. He was the kind of man you didn't mess with unless you were ready to play at his level. As she watched him, she couldn't shake the feeling that this might be the opportunity she'd been waiting for.

Big D leaned back in his chair, his eyes landing on Theresa. He watched her for a moment, a slow smile spreading across his face. She had something—an aura of determination mixed with a touch of desperation. She reminded him of himself back in the day, hungry for more, ready to take on the world.

He signaled to one of his men, who approached Theresa and whispered in her ear. "Big D wants to see you."

Theresa's heart skipped a beat. She took a deep breath and followed the man to the back of the bar. As she approached, Big D looked up, his gaze piercing.

"Theresa, right? Or should I call you Sugar?" Big D's voice was smooth, commanding.

"Either one works," Theresa replied, trying to keep her voice steady.

Big D gestured for her to sit. "I've been watchin' you. You got potential, girl. But you wastin' it on these streets."

Theresa sat down, her mind racing. "I'm doin' what I gotta do to survive. Ain't nobody gonna hand me nothin'."

Big D nodded, a glint of respect in his eyes. "That's the right attitude. But I'm talkin' 'bout more than just survivin'. I'm talkin' 'bout thrivin'. You got the looks, the brains, and the hustle. With my help, you could be more than just another girl on Backpage."

Theresa leaned forward, her curiosity piqued. "What you got in mind?"

Big D smiled, a predator's smile. "I can take you places you ain't never dreamed of. But it comes with a price. You work for me, you follow my rules. You ready to play at my level?"

Theresa weighed her options. She'd been hustling on her own for years, scraping by and dodging danger at every turn. Big D's offer was tempting, a chance to rise above the grind and claim something better. But she knew it wouldn't come easy.

"What's the catch?" she asked, her voice steady.

Big D's smile widened. "No catch. Just loyalty and hard work. You make me money, I make sure you get your cut. You cross me, you pay the price."

Theresa nodded, her decision made. "I'm in. What do I gotta do?"

Big D laid out the plan. He'd provide protection, connections, and clients willing to pay top dollar. In return, Theresa would work exclusively for him, bringing in money and expanding his empire. It was a partnership, but one where Big D held all the power.

Theresa agreed, seeing it as her best shot at changing her life. She knew the risks, but she was willing to take them. She'd play by Big D's rules, for now. But she kept her own plans close to her chest, determined to rise even higher.

Over the next few weeks, Big D's influence transformed Theresa's life. He set her up in a nicer apartment, away from the projects. He introduced her to high-rolling clients, men who were willing to pay for the best. She started making more money than she'd ever seen, her status rising along with her bank account.

But with the money came danger. Theresa learned quickly that Big D's world was ruthless. She had to watch her back, stay sharp, and trust no one. The streets might have been rough, but the world Big D introduced her to was a whole new level of cutthroat.

One night, as Theresa was getting ready for another job, she looked at herself in the mirror. She barely recognized the woman staring back at her. She was no longer the scared girl from the projects. She was Sugar, a force to be reckoned with.

Her phone buzzed, a message from Big D. "Got a big client tonight. Don't mess this up."

Theresa smirked, slipping on her heels. "I got this," she muttered to herself.

As she stepped out into the night, the air was electric with possibilities. She was on her way, climbing the ranks, playing the game. But she knew the stakes were high, and one wrong move could cost her everything.

Theresa met the client at an upscale hotel, her confidence masking the nerves underneath. The man was rich, powerful, and demanding. But she played her part perfectly, keeping him entertained and satisfied. When it was over, she counted the money, her mind already on the next step.

Back at her apartment, she poured herself a drink and sat on the balcony, looking out over the city. The lights twinkled below, each one a reminder of the world she was trying to conquer. She knew she couldn't let her guard down, not for a second.

Big D had given her an opportunity, but she had to prove herself every day. She had to stay one step ahead, always ready for the next challenge. The game was dangerous, but she was ready to play.

As she sipped her drink, her phone buzzed again. Another message from Big D. "Meet me tomorrow. Got a new assignment for you."

Theresa smiled, a thrill of excitement running through her. She was moving up, making her mark. But she couldn't forget where she came from, or the dangers that lurked around every corner.

The night was dark, the future uncertain. But Theresa was ready to face whatever came her way. She was determined to rise above, to claim her place in Big D's world. The stakes were high, but so were the rewards. And she was willing to gamble it all.

Chapter 3: Transformation Begins

Theresa stood in front of the full-length mirror in her new apartment, barely recognizing the woman staring back at her. Gone were the cheap clothes and tired eyes of a project escort. Big D had made sure she looked the part of a high-end escort, and the transformation was striking.

The past few weeks had been a whirlwind of change. Big D wasted no time in overhauling her appearance. He took her to upscale boutiques, where she tried on designer dresses, expensive heels, and luxurious lingerie. He brought in a top-notch stylist to revamp her hair, nails, and makeup. Theresa felt like a new woman, her confidence growing with each passing day.

"Look at you," Big D said, standing behind her as she admired herself in the mirror. "Ain't nobody gonna call you a project girl now. You ready to play with the big boys."

Theresa smiled, her eyes gleaming. "I'm ready, D. Let's do this."

The training began immediately. Big D was a seasoned pro, and he made sure Theresa understood every aspect of the game. They spent hours going over the rules, the dos and don'ts of the high-end escort business. He taught her how to spot dangerous clients, how to negotiate fees, and how to handle herself in any situation.

"You gotta be smart, Sugar," Big D said, his tone serious. "These men got money and power, but they also got secrets. You use that to your advantage."

Theresa listened intently, absorbing every word. She knew this was her shot at something better, and she wasn't going to waste it. Big D introduced her to his network, a web of influential clients, fellow escorts, and trusted allies. She learned who to trust and who to avoid, the subtle nuances of the business.

Her first few high-end clients were nerve-wracking, but Theresa quickly adapted. She played her role perfectly, exuding confidence and allure. The money flowed in, more than she'd ever made on Backpage.

She moved with a new sense of purpose, her every step a testament to her rising success.

One evening, Big D took her to an exclusive party in a penthouse suite, the kind of event she'd only ever seen in movies. The room was filled with the city's elite—politicians, businessmen, celebrities. Theresa felt a surge of adrenaline as she mingled, her charm and beauty turning heads.

"Remember, Sugar," Big D whispered in her ear. "You here to make connections. These people can take you places."

Theresa nodded, her eyes scanning the room. She approached a group of men, flashing them a dazzling smile. "Evening, gentlemen. Mind if I join you?"

They welcomed her into their circle, captivated by her presence. She flirted and laughed, all the while keeping her ears open for useful information. By the end of the night, she'd secured a few new clients and earned the respect of Big D's inner circle.

Theresa's success continued to soar. She upgraded her apartment to a sleek, modern loft in a better part of town. She no longer worried about bills or living paycheck to paycheck. The money was good, but more than that, she loved the power and respect she commanded.

One night, as she counted her earnings, Big D walked in, a satisfied smile on his face. "You doin' good, Sugar. Real good. But you gotta stay sharp. This life can turn on you in a heartbeat."

Theresa nodded, her eyes serious. "I know, D. I'm not gonna let my guard down."

Big D handed her a small package. "Here, open this."

Theresa unwrapped the package, revealing a diamond necklace. She gasped, her eyes wide with surprise. "D, this is beautiful."

"You earned it," he said, his voice low. "You keep this up, there's more where that came from. But remember, loyalty is everything."

Theresa slipped the necklace around her neck, feeling its weight. She looked at herself in the mirror, the diamonds sparkling against her skin.

She was no longer the scared girl from the projects. She was Sugar, a high-end escort with the world at her feet.

But success came with its own set of challenges. The higher she climbed, the more dangerous the game became. She had to navigate jealous rivals, demanding clients, and the constant threat of betrayal. She trusted Big D, but she also knew she had to watch her back. The streets had taught her that lesson well.

One evening, after a particularly lucrative night, she sat on her balcony, sipping champagne and looking out over the city. Her phone buzzed with a message from Big D. "New client tomorrow. Big fish. Don't screw it up."

Theresa smirked, typing back a quick reply. "I got this."

As she put down her phone, a sense of unease crept in. She was at the top of her game, but the stakes were higher than ever. One wrong move could bring everything crashing down. She took a deep breath, steeling herself for the challenges ahead. She was ready to play, ready to rise, but she couldn't shake the feeling that the game was just beginning.

The night was dark, the city alive with possibilities. Theresa was on her way up, but she knew she had to stay sharp, stay focused. The world she'd stepped into was glamorous but dangerous, filled with hidden traps and unseen enemies. She was determined to navigate it all, to rise above and claim her place at the top.

As she finished her champagne, she made a silent vow to herself. She would succeed, no matter what it took. She would play the game, and she would win. The future was hers for the taking, and she wasn't going to let anyone or anything stand in her way. The stakes were high, but so were the rewards. And Theresa was ready to gamble it all.

Chapter 4: New Status

Theresa strutted down the block, her heels clicking on the pavement, the summer sun bouncing off her diamond necklace. The hood watched as she passed by, heads turning, whispers following her every step. She wasn't just another girl from the projects anymore. She was the Hood Queen, and everyone knew it.

"Yo, that's Sugar," someone whispered as she walked by. "She rollin' with Big D now. Ain't nobody messin' with her."

Theresa smirked, her eyes scanning the familiar streets. She'd come a long way from those days hustling on Backpage just to get by. Now, she was a high-end escort, respected and feared. Her rise to the top had been quick, but the streets were always watching, waiting for any sign of weakness.

With her newfound status came a wave of jealousy and envy. The other escorts, women who had once been her friends, now saw her as a threat. The whispers started almost immediately, gossip spreading like wildfire.

"You hear 'bout Sugar? She think she all that 'cause she rollin' with Big D."

"Yeah, but how long she think that gonna last? She ain't special."

Theresa heard the whispers, felt the eyes on her back. She knew they were waiting for her to slip up, to fall from grace. But she wasn't about to give them the satisfaction.

One night, as she was getting ready for another high-profile client, her phone buzzed. It was Keisha, her best friend and confidante. "Yo, T, you gotta watch your back. These girls out here plottin' on you."

Theresa sighed, glancing at herself in the mirror. "I know, K. But they ain't got nothin' on me. I'm too smart for that."

Keisha's voice was filled with concern. "Just be careful. They jealous, and that makes 'em dangerous."

Theresa nodded, her resolve hardening. "I got this. Ain't nobody takin' me down."

Big D's influence over Theresa continued to grow as her success soared. He introduced her to more powerful clients, expanding her network and increasing her earnings. But with every new client, every new deal, his grip on her tightened.

"You doin' good, Sugar," he said one evening, his voice smooth and commanding. "But remember, you owe it all to me. Don't forget who put you where you are."

Theresa smiled, but there was an edge to it. "I know, D. I ain't forgettin'."

Big D nodded, satisfied. "Good. Keep it that way. You keep makin' me money, and we both stay on top."

Theresa played her part, always the loyal protégé. But deep down, she knew she had to watch her back. Big D was powerful, but he was also unpredictable. She couldn't afford to let her guard down, not for a second.

As her reputation grew, so did the envy and resentment from those around her. She walked through the hood with a target on her back, every step a challenge to those who wanted to see her fall. The gossip intensified, the plotting became more insidious.

One night, as she was leaving a client's penthouse, she was confronted by a group of women, led by Tasha, an old rival from her Backpage days. Tasha's eyes were filled with hatred, her voice dripping with venom.

"You think you better than us now, Sugar? Just 'cause you rollin' with Big D?"

Theresa held her ground, her eyes cold. "I earned my spot. Ain't nobody gave me nothin'. You got a problem with that?"

Tasha stepped closer, her fists clenched. "Yeah, I got a problem. You ain't nothin' but a jumped-up hoe, thinkin' you a queen. We gonna see how long you last."

Theresa's heart raced, but she didn't show her fear. "You best step off, Tasha. You don't want this fight."

The tension was palpable, the threat of violence hanging in the air. But before things could escalate, a car pulled up, and Big D's right-hand man, Reggie, stepped out.

"Yo, what's goin' on here?" Reggie's voice was loud, authoritative.

Tasha and her crew backed off, their eyes still filled with anger. "Nothin'," Tasha muttered, shooting Theresa a final glare before turning away.

Reggie nodded to Theresa. "You good?"

Theresa exhaled, her body relaxing slightly. "Yeah, I'm good. Thanks."

Reggie smirked. "Ain't no problem. Just keep doin' what you doin'. We got your back."

Despite the support from Big D and his crew, Theresa couldn't shake the feeling of unease. She knew she was walking a fine line, balancing her ambition with the constant threat of those who wanted to see her fail. The pressure was intense, but she thrived on it, using it to fuel her drive.

She spent her days meeting clients, closing deals, and expanding her empire. Her nights were filled with parties, networking events, and the ever-present danger of the streets. She was determined to stay on top, no matter what it took.

But the more successful she became, the more she realized just how deep Big D's control ran. He was always there, always watching, making sure she stayed in line. It was a partnership, but one where he held all the cards.

One evening, after a particularly lucrative night, Big D called her into his office. He leaned back in his chair, his eyes assessing her.

"You doin' good, Sugar. Real good. But don't forget, you play by my rules. You cross me, and it's over. Understand?"

Theresa nodded, her expression serious. "I understand, D. I ain't crossin' you."

Big D smiled, but it didn't reach his eyes. "Good. Keep it that way."

As Theresa left his office, she felt a mix of fear and determination. She was rising, making a name for herself, but the stakes were higher than ever. She had to stay sharp, stay focused, and never let her guard down.

The streets were unforgiving, but Theresa was ready for whatever came her way. She was the Hood Queen, and she wasn't going to let anyone take her crown. But she knew she had to be careful. One wrong move, and it could all come crashing down.

The night was dark, the future uncertain. But Theresa was ready to face whatever came next. She was determined to rise above, to claim her place at the top. The game was dangerous, but she was ready to play. And she wasn't going to let anyone stand in her way.

Chapter 5: Love and Betrayal

Theresa never thought she'd find herself tangled in the sheets with one of Big D's rivals, but life in the fast lane had a way of throwing unexpected curves. Ricky "Slim" Johnson was everything Big D wasn't—young, ambitious, and hungry for power. He had his eyes on Theresa from the moment he saw her, and it wasn't long before they fell into a passionate affair.

Their meetings were secret, conducted in dimly lit motels and secluded corners of the city. Slim was smooth with his words, his touch electrifying. He whispered promises of a life free from Big D's control, painting vivid pictures of the empire they could build together.

"You don't need him, Sugar," Slim murmured one night, his fingers tracing lazy circles on her back. "We can do this ourselves. We got the brains, the looks, and the hustle."

Theresa leaned into him, her mind a whirlwind of desire and ambition. "It ain't that simple, Slim. Big D's got connections. He'd come after us."

Slim's eyes glittered with determination. "We play it smart, we take him down from the inside. You got his trust. Use it. We can make this work."

Theresa knew she was playing a dangerous game, but the thrill of it was intoxicating. She started gathering information, listening closely during her meetings with Big D, storing away details that could be used against him. She was careful, meticulous, never letting on that her loyalties were shifting.

Slim's influence grew stronger with each passing day. He pushed her to take more risks, to dig deeper. Theresa found herself caught between two powerful men, her heart racing with the danger of it all. She knew she was on a tightrope, but she was determined to walk it.

One evening, after a particularly intense meeting with Big D, Theresa met Slim at their usual spot. He was waiting for her, his eyes dark with anticipation.

"You get anything new?" he asked, his voice low and urgent.

Theresa nodded, handing him a small notebook filled with notes. "This is everything. His clients, his contacts, the whole operation."

Slim's smile was triumphant. "We got him, Sugar. This is it."

The more Theresa and Slim plotted, the more confident she became. She started imagining a life where she wasn't under Big D's thumb, where she and Slim ruled the streets together. But the closer they got to their goal, the more dangerous the game became.

Big D wasn't a fool. He had eyes and ears everywhere. He started to notice the subtle changes in Theresa, the way she was more guarded, more secretive. He didn't confront her directly, but his suspicions grew.

Theresa felt the pressure mounting. She knew they were running out of time. One wrong move, and everything would come crashing down. She had to be perfect, had to outsmart Big D without him ever knowing.

One night, as she lay in bed with Slim, Theresa voiced her fears. "What if he finds out? What if he knows what we're doing?"

Slim pulled her close, his voice a soothing whisper. "He ain't gonna find out. We're too smart for that. We got this, Sugar."

Theresa wanted to believe him, but a nagging doubt lingered. She was in too deep, and there was no turning back. She had to see it through, no matter the cost.

The day of their planned takeover arrived. Slim had arranged for a group of his men to move in on Big D's territory, using the information Theresa had provided. It was a bold move, but one they hoped would catch Big D off guard.

Theresa sat in her apartment, her heart pounding as she waited for the call. The minutes dragged by, each one an eternity. Finally, her phone buzzed. It was Slim.

"It's done," he said, his voice filled with triumph. "We got his men, his clients. He's finished."

Theresa exhaled, relief washing over her. "What about Big D?"

Slim's tone darkened. "He got away. But it don't matter. We got everything else."

But the victory was short-lived. Big D wasn't one to go down without a fight. He retaliated swiftly and brutally, launching an all-out war on Slim and his men. The streets erupted into chaos, violence spilling over as the two sides clashed.

Theresa found herself in the middle of a nightmare. She'd played the game and now the consequences were raining down on her. She tried to stay calm, to navigate the storm, but the danger was everywhere.

One evening, as she was heading to meet Slim, she was ambushed. Big D's men grabbed her, dragging her into a dark alley. She fought, but they were too strong.

Big D emerged from the shadows, his eyes cold with fury. "Thought you could betray me, Sugar? Thought I wouldn't find out?"

Theresa's heart pounded, fear gripping her. "D, it ain't like that. I can explain."

Big D shook his head. "Save it. You made your choice."

The next few hours were a blur of violence and pain. Big D made it clear that betrayal had a price. When they finally let her go, Theresa was battered and broken, but her spirit remained uncrushed.

She stumbled to Slim's hideout, collapsing into his arms. "It's over, Slim. He knows."

Slim's face hardened. "Then we fight. We ain't givin' up."

Theresa nodded, her resolve steeling. They'd come too far to back down now. The game was still on, and she was more determined than ever to win.

As the night fell, Theresa and Slim prepared for the next move. The city was a battlefield, but she was ready to fight. She'd played her hand, and now it was time to see who would come out on top.

The night was dark, the stakes higher than ever. But Theresa Graham was ready for whatever came next. She was determined to rise above, to claim her place at the top. The game was dangerous, but she was ready to play. And she wasn't going to let anyone stand in her way.

Chapter 6: The Heist

Theresa sat in the dimly lit room, her eyes fixed on the blueprints spread out on the table. Slim was beside her, his fingers tracing the lines and notes they had meticulously prepared over the past few weeks. The plan was bold, risky, but if it worked, it would give them the upper hand against Big D.

"Alright, this is it," Slim said, his voice low and intense. "We hit his stash house tonight. It's the only way we can take him down and set up our own operation."

Theresa nodded, her heart pounding. "We gotta be quick, precise. In and out before he even knows what's happening."

Slim grinned, a dangerous glint in his eyes. "You ready for this, Sugar?"

Theresa met his gaze, determination burning in her chest. "Born ready. Let's do this."

The night was dark, the streets quiet. Theresa and Slim moved like shadows, slipping through alleyways and avoiding the watchful eyes of Big D's men. They reached the stash house, a nondescript building in the heart of Big D's territory. Slim's crew was already in position, waiting for the signal.

"Remember, we stick to the plan," Slim whispered, his hand brushing against Theresa's. "No mistakes."

Theresa nodded, her nerves on edge. She took a deep breath and focused. This was it—their chance to break free and carve out their own empire.

Slim signaled his crew, and they moved in. The front door was locked, but Slim had a guy for that. Skinny Pete, their tech wizard, worked quickly, picking the lock with practiced ease. The door clicked open, and they slipped inside, silent as ghosts.

The stash house was filled with cash, drugs, and weapons—everything Big D needed to maintain his grip on the streets.

Theresa and Slim split up, directing their crew to gather as much as they could carry. The atmosphere was tense, every sound magnified in the silence.

"Hurry up," Slim hissed, stuffing bundles of cash into a duffel bag. "We ain't got all night."

Theresa moved through the house, her eyes scanning for anything valuable. She found a safe in one of the back rooms and signaled Pete over. He worked his magic, the safe door swinging open to reveal stacks of money and a ledger filled with names and transactions.

"This is gold," Theresa whispered, grabbing the ledger. "We got him."

But as they were finishing up, the sound of footsteps echoed through the house. Theresa's heart skipped a beat. "We gotta go. Now."

They moved quickly, the tension palpable. Slim's crew filed out, bags full, but as they reached the front door, they were met with a group of Big D's men, guns drawn.

"Freeze!" one of them shouted, the barrel of his gun aimed at Theresa.

Slim reacted instinctively, pulling his own weapon and firing. The room erupted into chaos, bullets flying, shouts filling the air. Theresa ducked behind a couch, her heart racing. She returned fire, taking down one of Big D's men, but the situation was spiraling out of control.

"Fall back!" Slim yelled, grabbing Theresa's arm and pulling her towards the back door.

They scrambled through the house, the sound of gunfire following them. They burst out into the alley, running for their lives. Slim's crew scattered, trying to shake their pursuers.

They regrouped at a safe house, panting and covered in sweat. Slim paced the room, anger and frustration etched on his face. "How the hell did they know we were coming?"

Theresa shook her head, her mind racing. "I don't know. But we got what we came for."

Slim nodded, his eyes dark. "Yeah, but now he knows. We gotta move fast. Set up our operation before he comes after us."

Theresa agreed, but a sense of dread gnawed at her. They had made their move, but the game was far from over. Big D wouldn't take this betrayal lightly, and they had to be ready for whatever came next.

The news of the heist spread quickly. Big D's fury was palpable, his men combing the streets for any sign of Theresa and Slim. The tension in the hood rose to a boiling point, everyone on edge, waiting for the next explosion of violence.

Theresa and Slim worked tirelessly, setting up their own operation. They recruited loyal soldiers, secured new clients, and fortified their territory. But the specter of Big D loomed large, his wrath a constant threat.

One night, as they were finalizing their plans, Theresa's phone buzzed. It was a message from an unknown number: "You think you can take what's mine and walk away? This ain't over."

Her blood ran cold, her fingers tightening around the phone. She showed the message to Slim, his jaw clenching with anger.

"He's coming for us," Slim said, his voice deadly calm. "We gotta be ready."

The following days were a blur of preparation. Theresa couldn't shake the feeling of impending doom, but she pushed through, her resolve unyielding. She had made her choice, and there was no turning back.

Big D's retaliation came swiftly. His men launched a series of attacks on their territory, the streets erupting into chaos. Theresa and Slim fought back, their operation holding strong, but the cost was high. Lives were lost, and the violence seemed never-ending.

As the dust settled, Theresa knew they were in for the fight of their lives. The heist had been a bold move, but now they had to face the consequences. Big D was a formidable enemy, and he wouldn't rest until they were destroyed.

Theresa stood on the balcony of their hideout, looking out over the city. The night was dark, the future uncertain. But she was ready. She had played the game, and now it was time to see it through.

"We got this," Slim said, coming up behind her. "We're gonna take him down, once and for all."

Theresa nodded, her eyes steely with determination. "Yeah, we are. But we gotta be smart, gotta be ruthless."

The game was dangerous, but Theresa was ready for whatever came next. She was determined to rise above, to claim her place at the top. The stakes were higher than ever, but she was willing to gamble it all. And she wasn't going to let anyone stand in her way.

Chapter 7: Confrontation

The tension in the air was thick enough to cut with a knife. Theresa paced the floor of the safe house, her nerves on edge. The heist had gone down, but the repercussions were hitting hard. Big D's retaliation had been swift and brutal. The streets were buzzing with whispers and fear, everyone waiting for the next move.

She glanced at Slim, who was on the phone, barking orders to his crew. "We gotta tighten security. Big D ain't playin' no more. He's comin' for blood."

Slim nodded, his face set in a grim mask. "I know. We gotta be ready for whatever he throws at us."

But even as they fortified their defenses, Theresa couldn't shake the feeling that something big was coming. She felt it in her bones, a storm brewing on the horizon.

That night, the confrontation came. Big D stormed into their territory, flanked by his men, his eyes blazing with fury. Theresa stood her ground, Slim and their crew at her side. The two factions faced off, the tension crackling like electricity.

"Theresa!" Big D's voice boomed, filled with anger. "You think you can steal from me and get away with it?"

Theresa met his gaze, her heart pounding but her face betraying no fear. "I did what I had to do, D. You ain't the only one tryin' to survive out here."

Big D's eyes narrowed, his fists clenched at his sides. "You crossed the line, girl. And now you gonna pay."

The air was charged with danger, both sides poised for violence. Slim stepped forward, his voice low and deadly. "We ain't backin' down, D. You come at us, you better be ready for a fight."

Big D's response was swift. He pulled a gun from his waistband, aiming it at Slim. "You really think you can take me on, boy? You ain't nothin' but a punk."

The words were barely out of his mouth when the first shot rang out. Chaos erupted, both sides diving for cover as bullets flew. Theresa ducked behind a car, her heart racing as she returned fire. The sound of gunfire filled the air, mingling with shouts and screams.

She saw Slim go down, clutching his side, blood seeping through his fingers. "Slim!" she screamed, crawling towards him.

He looked up at her, his face pale but determined. "I'm good, Sugar. Just keep fightin'."

Theresa's vision blurred with rage. She turned her attention back to the fight, her gun blazing. She took down two of Big D's men, her mind focused on one thing: survival.

The battle raged on, but slowly, Big D's men began to retreat. They hadn't expected such fierce resistance. Big D himself was the last to back off, his eyes still locked on Theresa.

"This ain't over," he snarled, backing away. "You hear me? This ain't over!"

The aftermath was brutal. Slim was rushed to the safe house, where Theresa did her best to patch him up. He was pale and sweating, but he managed a weak smile. "We did good, Sugar. We held our ground."

Theresa nodded, her hands trembling as she cleaned his wound. "Yeah, but this is just the start. He's gonna come back, harder than before."

Slim's eyes hardened. "Then we'll be ready. We ain't givin' up."

As the night wore on, Theresa couldn't sleep. She sat by Slim's side, her mind racing. The confrontation had been a wake-up call. Big D wasn't going to let them take over without a fight, and the streets were about to get even bloodier.

But despite the danger, despite the bloodshed, Theresa's resolve only grew stronger. She was in this for the long haul, and she wasn't about to back down.

In the following days, Theresa and Slim fortified their operation. They recruited more men, secured more territory, and prepared for the inevitable counterattack. The streets buzzed with tension, everyone waiting for the next explosion of violence.

Theresa moved like a queen, her head held high, her eyes sharp. She knew Big D was watching, waiting for her to slip. But she wasn't going to give him the satisfaction.

One evening, as she stood on the balcony of their hideout, Slim joined her. His wound was healing, but the fire in his eyes was undiminished.

"We gotta keep pushin," he said, his voice firm. "Big D ain't gonna stop, and neither are we."

Theresa nodded, her gaze fixed on the city below. "We'll take him down, Slim. We'll take everything."

The night was dark, the future uncertain. But Theresa was ready for whatever came next. She had faced Big D's fury and come out stronger. The game was far from over, but she was determined to win. The stakes were higher than ever, but so were the rewards. And Theresa was willing to gamble it all.

As the city buzzed with rumors and fear, Theresa knew one thing for sure: the fight had just begun. She was ready for the battles ahead, ready to face whatever came her way. The game was dangerous, but she was a player, and she wasn't going to let anyone stand in her way. The streets were unforgiving, but so was she. And as long as she had Slim by her side, she knew they could take on the world.

The night was dark, the air thick with tension. But Theresa was ready. She had faced Big D and survived. Now, it was time to take him down for good. The game was on, and she was in it to win it.

Chapter 8: Power Struggle

The streets were a battlefield. Theresa and Big D were locked in a relentless war for control, and the hood was caught in the crossfire. Territory was everything, and each block, each corner, became a prize to be fought over with blood and bullets.

Theresa stood in the middle of the street, her crew surrounding her, ready for action. The sun was setting, casting long shadows that seemed to deepen the tension hanging in the air.

"Alright, y'all," Theresa said, her voice low but commanding. "We takin' the east side tonight. Big D's got his men there, but we gonna push 'em out. This is our turf now."

Slim, still healing from his wound but as determined as ever, nodded. "We hit hard and fast. Don't give 'em a chance to regroup."

The crew was ready. They moved with purpose, slipping through alleyways and cutting across vacant lots. They knew the streets better than anyone, and they used that knowledge to their advantage.

The first shots rang out as they approached the east side. Big D's men were there, just as they expected, but Theresa's crew was prepared. A fierce firefight erupted, the crack of gunfire echoing through the night. Theresa ducked behind a car, returning fire, her heart pounding.

"Push forward!" she shouted, her voice cutting through the chaos. "Don't let 'em hold us back!"

Her crew advanced, methodically taking down their opponents. The streets were filled with shouts, the smell of gunpowder, and the flicker of muzzle flashes. It was brutal, but Theresa's resolve never wavered. She was fighting for her future, for control, and she wasn't about to back down.

As the battle raged, Theresa knew she needed more than just brute force. She needed alliances, people she could trust to stand by her side. She reached out to old contacts, making deals and promises, pulling in favors she'd earned over the years.

One night, she met with Rico, a former rival who had his own gripes with Big D. They sat in a dimly lit bar, the air thick with tension and smoke.

"Rico, I need your help," Theresa said, cutting straight to the point. "You got men, resources. We join forces, we can take Big D down."

Rico leaned back, studying her. "Why should I trust you, Sugar? We ain't exactly been friends."

Theresa's eyes were hard. "This ain't about friendship. It's about business. Big D's got too much power. We take him down, we split his territory. We both win."

Rico considered for a moment, then nodded. "Alright. I'm in. But don't think for a second I won't turn on you if you cross me."

Theresa smirked. "I wouldn't expect anything less."

With new allies came new enemies. Word of Theresa's rise spread quickly, and those who once saw her as just another player now viewed her as a threat. The streets buzzed with rumors, plots, and whispers of betrayal.

One evening, as she was walking back to her hideout, Theresa felt eyes on her. She turned just in time to see a group of men approaching, their intentions clear. She reached for her gun, ready to defend herself, but they struck fast, overwhelming her.

They dragged her into an alley, the leader sneering down at her. "Big D sends his regards. He says you been a thorn in his side for too long."

Theresa struggled, spitting at the man's feet. "Tell D he can come see me himself if he's got a problem."

The man raised his fist, but before he could strike, a gunshot rang out. Slim and her crew had arrived, driving off her attackers. Theresa stood, wiping blood from her lip, her eyes blazing with fury.

"We gotta hit back, harder," she said, her voice shaking with anger. "We take the fight to him. Show him we ain't scared."

The power struggle escalated. The violence grew more intense, the stakes higher. Each confrontation left more bodies in the streets, the air thick with tension and fear. The hood was divided, everyone forced to pick a side.

Theresa's alliances held, but just barely. Trust was a rare commodity, and betrayal was always a heartbeat away. She moved with caution, always watching her back, knowing that any misstep could be her last.

One night, as she sat with Slim, going over their next move, he looked at her, his eyes filled with concern. "We're in deep, Sugar. You sure we can pull this off?"

Theresa met his gaze, her resolve unshaken. "We ain't got no choice, Slim. It's win or die. And I ain't planning on dying."

Slim nodded, a grim smile on his lips. "Then we fight. And we don't stop until Big D's outta the picture."

The final showdown was inevitable. The streets were a powder keg, ready to explode. Theresa and her crew prepared for the biggest battle yet, their nerves steeled for the fight ahead.

As they moved into position, the tension was palpable. The night was dark, the air heavy with anticipation. Theresa's heart pounded, but her mind was clear. She was ready.

Big D's men were waiting, and as the first shots rang out, chaos erupted. The battle was fierce, each side fighting with everything they had. Theresa moved through the fray, her gun blazing, her eyes fixed on her goal.

She saw Big D across the battlefield, his eyes locked on hers. This was it. The final confrontation. The culmination of everything they'd fought for.

The fight was brutal, the casualties mounting. But Theresa pushed forward, her determination unyielding. She would not back down. She would not be defeated.

As the dust settled, the streets were eerily quiet. The battle was over, but the war was far from won. Theresa stood amidst the wreckage, her breath coming in ragged gasps. She had survived, but the cost was high.

Slim approached her, his face grim. "We did it. We pushed them back."

Theresa nodded, her eyes scanning the battlefield. "Yeah. But this ain't the end. Big D's still out there. And he's gonna come back, harder than ever."

Slim's eyes hardened. "Then we'll be ready. We ain't stoppin' now."

The night was dark, the future uncertain. But Theresa was ready for whatever came next. The power struggle was far from over, but she was determined to win. The stakes were higher than ever, but so were the rewards. And Theresa was willing to gamble it all.

As the city buzzed with the aftermath of the battle, Theresa knew one thing for sure: the fight had just begun. She was ready for the battles ahead, ready to face whatever came her way. The streets were unforgiving, but so was she. And as long as she had Slim by her side, she knew they could take on the world.

The game was dangerous, but Theresa was a player, and she wasn't going to let anyone stand in her way. The streets were her battlefield, and she was ready to fight. The power struggle was on, and she was in it to win it.

Chapter 9: Under Pressure

Theresa sat in her office, the tension in the air palpable. The room was filled with the hum of voices, her crew discussing their next moves, but her mind was elsewhere. The pressure was mounting from all sides, and she could feel the walls closing in.

"Yo, Sugar," Slim said, snapping her out of her thoughts. "We got a problem. The cops are steppin' up their game. They been raiding spots all over the city."

Theresa's heart sank. She'd heard the rumors, but hearing it confirmed was different. "What's their angle?"

Slim shook his head. "They got new orders to crack down on all escort operations. Big D's in their sights, but that means we're on their radar too."

Theresa leaned back in her chair, her mind racing. "We need to lay low, move our operations underground. But we can't stop. We got too much at stake."

The next few days were a whirlwind of activity. Theresa and Slim worked tirelessly to relocate their business, using safe houses and encrypted communications to stay one step ahead of the law. But the constant threat of police raids loomed over them, a dark cloud that never lifted.

One night, as Theresa was going over plans with Slim, her phone buzzed. It was a message from Keisha, her best friend and confidante. "We got a snitch. Someone's been leaking info to the cops."

Theresa's blood ran cold. "Who?"

Keisha's response was swift. "Don't know yet. But we need to find out before it's too late."

Theresa's mind raced. Betrayal from within was the last thing she needed. She called a meeting with her top lieutenants, her eyes scanning each face for signs of guilt.

"We got a rat," she said, her voice cold. "Whoever's been feeding info to the cops, I'm gonna find you. And when I do, you're done."

The room was silent, the tension thick. Theresa knew she had to act fast. The longer the snitch remained hidden, the greater the risk to her operation.

As the pressure mounted, so did the cracks in her organization. Trust was eroding, suspicion creeping into every interaction. Theresa's lieutenants started eyeing each other with distrust, the strain taking its toll.

One night, as she was checking on one of their safe houses, Theresa caught one of her men, Marcus, trying to slip away with a bag of cash. Her anger flared.

"Marcus! What the hell you think you doin'?" she shouted, blocking his path.

Marcus's eyes were wide with fear. "I was just— I needed—"

Theresa grabbed him by the collar, her voice low and dangerous. "You think you can steal from me? After everything I've done for you?"

Marcus stammered, his fear palpable. "I'm sorry, Sugar. I swear, it won't happen again."

Theresa's grip tightened. "Damn right it won't. Get outta my sight before I change my mind."

As Marcus fled, Theresa felt a wave of exhaustion wash over her. She was fighting battles on all fronts, and it was wearing her down. The constant pressure was taking its toll, and she knew she had to find a way to regain control.

The police raids continued, each one hitting closer to home. Theresa's nerves were frayed, her once-steady hands now trembling with anxiety. She couldn't afford to make mistakes, but the stakes were higher than ever.

One evening, Slim burst into her office, his face pale. "Sugar, they got Keisha. The cops raided her spot. They're squeezin' her for info."

Theresa's heart skipped a beat. "We gotta get her out. If she talks—"

Slim nodded. "I know. But we gotta be smart. We can't just bust in there."

Theresa's mind raced, desperate for a solution. She couldn't lose Keisha. Not now. "We need a distraction. Something big to draw the cops' attention."

Slim's eyes lit up. "I got an idea. It's risky, but it might just work."

That night, they set their plan in motion. Slim's crew staged a series of high-profile heists across the city, drawing the police away from Keisha's location. The plan was dangerous, but it was their only shot.

As the chaos unfolded, Theresa and Slim moved in, slipping past the distracted officers to reach Keisha. They found her in a holding cell, her eyes wide with relief when she saw them.

"About damn time," Keisha muttered as Slim picked the lock.

Theresa pulled her into a tight hug. "We gotta move. They'll be back any minute."

They slipped out, moving quickly through the shadows. The streets were alive with sirens and flashing lights, but they managed to stay one step ahead.

Back at the safe house, Theresa felt a moment of reprieve. Keisha was safe, but the pressure was still mounting. The police weren't going to back off, and the internal conflicts within her organization were growing.

She sat with Slim and Keisha, exhaustion etched on her face. "We need to find that snitch. And we need to do it fast."

Keisha nodded, her expression grim. "I'll start digging. But we need to be careful. Trust is a rare commodity right now."

Theresa sighed, her mind heavy with the weight of her decisions. "We'll figure it out. We always do."

The days that followed were a blur of tension and uncertainty. Theresa moved like a queen under siege, always watching, always waiting for the next threat. The pressure from the police and the internal strife were pushing her to her limits, but she refused to break.

One night, as she stood on the balcony of their hideout, Slim joined her. His presence was a comfort, a reminder that she wasn't alone in this fight.

"We'll get through this, Sugar," he said softly. "We've faced worse."

Theresa nodded, her resolve hardening. "I know. But we gotta stay sharp. The game's changed, and we need to adapt."

Slim's eyes were filled with determination. "We will. We always do."

The night was dark, the future uncertain. But Theresa was ready for whatever came next. She had faced the pressure, the betrayal, and the constant threat of the law, and she was still standing. The stakes were higher than ever, but so were the rewards. And Theresa was willing to gamble it all.

As the city buzzed with the aftermath of their latest moves, Theresa knew one thing for sure: the fight was far from over. She was ready for the battles ahead, ready to face whatever came her way. The streets were unforgiving, but so was she. And as long as she had Slim and Keisha by her side, she knew they could take on the world.

The game was dangerous, but Theresa was a player, and she wasn't going to let anyone stand in her way. The pressure was on, but she was ready to fight. The struggle was real, but so was her determination. The game was on, and she was in it to win it.

Chapter 10: Personal Costs

Theresa was sitting in her office, staring at the phone on her desk. The tension in the room was thick, the air heavy with unspoken fears. She'd been through hell lately, dodging the cops, dealing with betrayal, and holding her operation together by sheer force of will. But nothing prepared her for the call she was about to make.

She picked up the phone and dialed her mom's number. It rang twice before she heard the familiar voice.

"Hey, Ma," Theresa said, trying to keep her voice steady. "How you doin'?"

"Theresa, it's been a minute. I'm hangin' in there. How about you, baby?"

Theresa closed her eyes, the sound of her mother's voice tugging at her heart. "I'm good, Ma. Just busy, you know? I wanted to check on you, make sure everything's alright."

Her mother sighed. "We're gettin' by. But you know, it'd be nice to see you more often. Your sister's been askin' about you."

Theresa's heart ached. She missed her family, but her life had become a whirlwind of danger and deceit. "I know, Ma. I'll try to visit soon. I promise."

Later that night, as she sat alone in her apartment, the weight of her choices pressed down on her. The streets had claimed so much of her life, and now it felt like they were closing in on her family too. She knew she was walking a dangerous path, but she couldn't turn back now.

The next day, as she was going over plans with Slim, her phone buzzed. It was her younger sister, Shaniqua. The urgency in her voice was palpable.

"Theresa, you need to come home. Ma's hurt."

Theresa's heart skipped a beat. "What happened?"

"Some guys came by, lookin' for you. They trashed the place, and Ma got caught in the middle. She's in the hospital."

Theresa's blood ran cold. "I'm on my way."

She turned to Slim, her face set in grim determination. "I gotta go. My family's in trouble."

Slim nodded, concern etched on his face. "You need backup?"

Theresa shook her head. "No. This is personal."

The hospital was a blur of sterile smells and anxious faces. Theresa found her mother in a small, dimly lit room, hooked up to monitors and IVs. Shaniqua was sitting beside the bed, her eyes red from crying.

"Ma," Theresa whispered, her voice breaking.

Her mother opened her eyes, weak but aware. "Theresa, baby. You came."

Tears streamed down Theresa's face. "I'm so sorry, Ma. This is all my fault."

Her mother's hand reached out, gripping hers tightly. "You doin' what you gotta do. Just be careful, baby. I don't wanna lose you."

Theresa nodded, her heart breaking. She knew she had to protect her family, but the cost was tearing her apart.

The days that followed were filled with a sense of impending doom. Theresa's mother recovered slowly, but the damage was done. The attack had been a message, a brutal reminder that her enemies would stop at nothing to get to her.

Theresa's mind was a whirlwind of emotions. She felt the weight of her choices pressing down on her, the lines between right and wrong blurring. She had built her empire on grit and determination, but now it felt like everything was slipping through her fingers.

One night, as she sat alone in her apartment, her thoughts turned dark. She wondered if it was all worth it—the money, the power, the constant danger. She had sacrificed so much, but at what cost?

Her phone buzzed, breaking her from her thoughts. It was Keisha, her voice filled with concern. "Theresa, we need to talk. People are startin' to question your leadership."

Theresa's heart sank. "What do you mean?"

Keisha sighed. "Some of the crew think you're losin' your edge. They're worried about the cops, the attacks. They think maybe it's time for a change."

Theresa's blood boiled. "Who's sayin' that?"

Keisha hesitated. "I don't wanna name names, but you need to get a grip on things. Fast."

The pressure was mounting from all sides. Theresa felt isolated, her once-loyal friends and allies starting to distance themselves. The fear of betrayal hung heavy in the air, trust eroding with each passing day.

One evening, as she walked through the neighborhood, she felt eyes on her. Whispers followed her every step, the streets filled with rumors and suspicion. She knew she had to take control, but the weight of her decisions was crushing her.

She found Slim at their hideout, his face lined with worry. "Sugar, we gotta talk."

Theresa sat down, her eyes weary. "What now?"

Slim sighed. "We got problems. The crew's restless, the cops are closing in, and Big D ain't lettin' up. We need to make some hard decisions."

Theresa nodded, her resolve hardening. "I know. But we gotta stick together. We can't let 'em see us break."

Slim's eyes softened. "I'm with you, Sugar. Always. But we need a plan."

Theresa spent the night strategizing, her mind racing with possibilities. She knew she had to regain control, to show her strength. But the personal cost was tearing her apart. She missed her family, missed the simple life she'd once had. But there was no turning back now.

As the first light of dawn broke, Theresa stood on her balcony, looking out over the city. The streets were quiet, the calm before the storm. She knew the battle ahead would be brutal, but she was ready.

She turned to Slim, her eyes steely with determination. "We're gonna take control. We're gonna show 'em who's boss. And we're gonna do it together."

Slim nodded, his face set with resolve. "Let's do this."

The night was dark, the future uncertain. But Theresa was ready for whatever came next. The personal costs were high, but she was determined to rise above. The stakes were higher than ever, but so were the rewards. And Theresa was willing to gamble it all.

As the city buzzed with tension and fear, Theresa knew one thing for sure: the fight was far from over. She was ready for the battles ahead, ready to face whatever came her way. The streets were unforgiving, but so was she. And as long as she had Slim by her side, she knew they could take on the world.

The game was dangerous, but Theresa was a player, and she wasn't going to let anyone stand in her way. The personal costs were real, but so was her determination. The game was on, and she was in it to win it.

Chapter 11: Big D's Revenge

Theresa stood in the heart of her territory, feeling the tension in the air. The streets were quiet, too quiet, like the calm before a storm. She knew Big D wasn't done with her, not by a long shot. He was plotting, waiting for the right moment to strike back and reclaim his power.

One evening, as she was meeting with Slim to discuss their next move, her phone buzzed. It was a message from an unknown number: "You think you safe? Think again."

Theresa showed the message to Slim, her jaw clenched. "Big D's makin' his move. We need to be ready."

Slim nodded, his face set in a grim expression. "We gotta tighten security. No one gets in or out without us knowin.'"

But despite their precautions, Big D was always one step ahead. He had connections, people in high places, and a devious mind that never stopped scheming. He knew how to play the game, and he was about to play it to perfection.

Late one night, Theresa and her crew were wrapping up a meeting when a sudden commotion erupted outside. Sirens wailed, and the flashing red and blue lights of police cars filled the streets.

"Shit," Slim muttered, grabbing his gun. "Cops are here."

Theresa's heart pounded. "We gotta move, now!"

But before they could escape, the door was kicked in, and officers flooded the room, guns drawn. "Hands in the air! Nobody move!"

Theresa felt a sinking feeling in her stomach. They'd been set up. She complied, raising her hands, her mind racing. Who had betrayed them? How had Big D managed this?

The officers moved in, cuffing everyone. Theresa was pushed to the ground, her face pressed against the cold floor. She could hear Slim shouting, protesting, but it was no use. They were caught.

As they were hauled out to the waiting police cars, Theresa caught sight of Big D standing in the shadows, a smug smile on his face. He tipped his hat to her, his eyes gleaming with victory.

"Enjoyin' the show, Sugar?" he called out. "This is what happens when you cross me."

Theresa's rage boiled over, but she was powerless. The doors slammed shut, and the car sped off, taking her to a place she'd never wanted to see again—jail.

The jail was a harsh, unforgiving place. Theresa was stripped of her dignity, her power, and thrown into a cell with hardened criminals. The walls closed in on her, the reality of her situation hitting hard. She was no longer the queen of the streets. Here, she was just another inmate, another number.

Days turned into weeks, each one a battle for survival. Theresa kept to herself, her mind focused on one thing: getting out and taking her revenge on Big D. But the monotony, the constant threat of violence, wore her down.

One day, as she sat in the yard, a group of inmates approached her. Their leader, a tall, muscular woman with cold eyes, sneered down at her. "So you're the famous Sugar. Heard a lot about you."

Theresa met her gaze, refusing to show fear. "Yeah? What of it?"

The woman laughed, a harsh, grating sound. "You ain't so tough in here, are you? Word is, Big D put you here. That true?"

Theresa's eyes narrowed. "What's it to you?"

The woman shrugged. "Just curious. But let me give you some advice—keep your head down. You ain't in control here."

Theresa didn't respond, her mind whirling with plans. She couldn't afford to get into trouble, not if she wanted to get out. But she wouldn't back down either. She had to stay strong, stay focused.

Life behind bars was a constant struggle. The guards were corrupt, the inmates ruthless. Theresa learned quickly who to trust and who to avoid. She kept her head down, doing her time, but never stopped thinking about the outside, about Big D and the revenge she would take.

She received visits from Keisha and Slim, their faces a lifeline in the grim reality of jail. They updated her on the situation outside, the constant battle for control.

"Big D's tightening his grip," Slim said during one visit. "But we ain't givin' up. We're keepin' the fight alive."

Theresa's eyes burned with determination. "Good. Keep the pressure on him. I'll be out soon, and when I am, we're takin' him down."

Keisha squeezed her hand, her eyes filled with concern. "Just stay safe, T. We need you out here."

The days dragged on, each one blending into the next. Theresa counted the days, each one bringing her closer to her release. She used the time to plan, to think about every move she'd make once she was free.

One evening, as she lay in her bunk, the cell block quiet, she heard a commotion. She sat up, listening intently. The guards were moving through the cells, calling out names.

"Theresa Graham!"

Her heart leapt. Was it time? She quickly got up, her mind racing. The guard opened her cell, a smirk on his face. "Pack your stuff. You're out."

Theresa didn't wait to be told twice. She gathered her things, her heart pounding with anticipation. She walked out of the cell, her eyes steely with resolve. This wasn't the end. It was just the beginning.

As she stepped outside, the fresh air hit her like a wave. Keisha and Slim were waiting, their faces breaking into smiles as they saw her.

"Welcome back, Sugar," Slim said, pulling her into a hug.

Theresa hugged him back, her mind already racing with plans. "Thanks. Now let's get to work."

Keisha handed her a phone. "We kept everything going, but it's been tough. Big D's got more power than ever."

Theresa's eyes hardened. "Not for long. We're takin' him down."

The ride back to their territory was filled with updates and plans. Theresa listened, her mind sharp, her resolve unbreakable. She had been knocked down, but she wasn't out. She was back, and she was ready to reclaim her throne.

The night was dark, the city alive with possibilities. Theresa was ready for whatever came next. The game was on, and she was in it to win it. The stakes were higher than ever, but so were the rewards. And Theresa was willing to gamble it all.

As the car sped through the city, Theresa looked out at the streets she knew so well. The fight was far from over, but she was ready. She had faced Big D's revenge and come out stronger. Now, it was time for her to strike back. The game was dangerous, but Theresa was a player, and she wasn't going to let anyone stand in her way.

The night was dark, but the future was hers for the taking. She was ready to fight, ready to reclaim her power. The game was on, and she was in it to win it.

Chapter 12: Survival in Jail

Theresa quickly learned that jail was a whole new kind of jungle. The walls were high, the air was thick with despair, and the sounds of clanging metal and distant shouts echoed through the hallways. Survival here meant navigating the brutal politics of prison life, where every move could be a matter of life and death.

The first day was the hardest. She was thrown into a cell block with hardened criminals, women who had been through hell and back. Theresa had to adapt fast, her street smarts kicking into high gear. She kept her head down, observing, learning the unspoken rules of this new world.

One morning, as she sat in the mess hall, she felt eyes on her. The leader of the block, a woman named Big Mama, was watching her. Big Mama was a towering figure, respected and feared by everyone. She ran the place with an iron fist, and her approval could mean the difference between survival and suffering.

Theresa decided to make her move. She walked over to Big Mama's table, her heart pounding but her face calm. "Mind if I sit?"

Big Mama looked her up and down, a slow smile spreading across her face. "So, you the famous Sugar. Heard you was a boss on the outside."

Theresa met her gaze, unflinching. "I was. And I can be useful in here too."

Big Mama chuckled. "Bold. I like that. Sit down, let's talk."

Theresa quickly realized that forming alliances was crucial. She started by earning Big Mama's respect, showing her that she could handle herself. She proved her worth by helping with various tasks, from smuggling contraband to settling disputes. In return, Big Mama offered protection, making sure no one messed with her.

But jailhouse politics were tricky. Trust was a rare commodity, and betrayal was always a possibility. Theresa kept her circle tight, only confiding in a few trusted inmates. One of them was Latoya, a tough but loyal woman who had been inside for years.

"Yo, Sugar," Latoya said one night as they sat in the yard. "Word is, you got beef with Big D on the outside. That true?"

Theresa nodded, her jaw clenched. "He set me up. Took everything I built. I'm gonna take him down, soon as I'm out."

Latoya's eyes gleamed with interest. "You need people on the outside for that. You got a plan?"

Theresa's mind raced. She had been thinking about revenge every day since she got locked up. "I got some ideas. But I need connections. You got anyone who can help?"

Latoya grinned. "I might. But it'll cost you."

Theresa nodded. "Whatever it takes. Just make it happen."

The days turned into weeks, and Theresa continued to navigate the dangerous waters of jailhouse politics. She built alliances, forming a network of women who had her back. Together, they shared information, protected each other, and planned for the future.

One night, as they sat in the dimly lit cell block, Theresa gathered her closest allies. "We need to get word to my crew on the outside. I need them to start setting things up for when I get out."

Big Mama leaned in, her eyes sharp. "You got a message?"

Theresa nodded. "Yeah. Tell Slim to keep the pressure on Big D. Don't let up, not for a second. And tell Keisha to keep recruiting. We need as many people as we can get."

Big Mama smiled. "Consider it done."

Life in jail was harsh, but Theresa adapted. She learned to navigate the power dynamics, using her wits and her alliances to stay ahead. But the constant threat of violence was always there, a shadow hanging over her every move.

One day, as she was walking back to her cell, she was ambushed by a group of inmates. They shoved her into a corner, their faces twisted with malice.

"You think you're tough, Sugar?" one of them sneered. "Big D's got people everywhere. You ain't safe, even in here."

Theresa's heart raced, but she refused to show fear. "You got a message for me? Tell Big D I'm comin' for him."

The leader of the group lunged at her, but before she could land a blow, Latoya and Big Mama's crew arrived, pulling them apart.

"Back off," Big Mama growled. "Sugar's under my protection. You mess with her, you mess with me."

The attackers backed down, their eyes filled with hatred. Theresa knew she had made powerful enemies, but she also had powerful allies.

As the weeks turned into months, Theresa's resolve never wavered. She spent every spare moment planning her revenge, her mind a whirlwind of schemes and strategies. She knew she had to be smart, had to outthink Big D at every turn.

One evening, as she sat in her cell, a guard approached. "Graham, you got a visitor."

Theresa's heart leapt. It was Slim. She followed the guard to the visitation room, her mind racing with questions.

Slim looked rough, but his eyes were bright with determination. "We're keepin' things together out there, Sugar. Just like you said. But it's tough. Big D's makin' moves."

Theresa nodded. "We gotta stay strong. I'm workin' on some things in here. We'll take him down, Slim. I promise."

Slim squeezed her hand. "We're with you, Sugar. All the way."

The visit reinvigorated Theresa. She returned to her cell with renewed determination, her mind sharp and focused. She knew the road ahead was long and dangerous, but she was ready for the fight.

As the days passed, she continued to build her alliances, strengthen her network, and plan for the future. She knew that every moment she spent behind bars was one step closer to her revenge.

The night was dark, the future uncertain. But Theresa was ready for whatever came next. She had faced the brutal realities of jail and come out stronger. The game was far from over, but she was determined to win. The stakes were higher than ever, but so were the rewards. And Theresa was willing to gamble it all.

As the city buzzed with tension and fear, Theresa knew one thing for sure: the fight was far from over. She was ready for the battles ahead, ready to face whatever came her way. The streets were unforgiving, but so was she. And as long as she had her allies by her side, she knew they could take on the world.

The game was dangerous, but Theresa was a player, and she wasn't going to let anyone stand in her way. The struggle was real, but so was her determination. The game was on, and she was in it to win it.

Chapter 13: Release and Revenge

The steel gates of the prison clanged open, and Theresa stepped out into the harsh sunlight, squinting as her eyes adjusted to the brightness. The air felt different, fresher, filled with possibilities. She was free, but the battle was far from over. She was out on bail, and every moment counted. She had one goal: to take down Big D.

Slim was waiting for her, leaning against a sleek black car. He looked up, a slow smile spreading across his face as he saw her. "Welcome back, Sugar. We got work to do."

Theresa nodded, her resolve hardening. "Damn right we do. Let's get to it."

Rebuilding her life wasn't easy. The streets had changed while she was inside, and she had to reestablish her presence, remind people who she was and what she was capable of. She started by reconnecting with her old crew, solidifying alliances, and recruiting new blood.

The first few days were a blur of meetings and strategy sessions. Theresa moved like a woman possessed, her mind racing with plans and possibilities. She knew she couldn't afford to waste time. Big D was still out there, tightening his grip on the streets, and she had to act fast.

One evening, as she sat in her new apartment, Slim brought her up to speed. "Big D's been makin' moves, Sugar. He's got new suppliers, more muscle. He thinks he's untouchable."

Theresa smirked, a dangerous glint in her eyes. "He's about to find out just how wrong he is."

Theresa's plan was simple but deadly. She needed to hit Big D where it hurt—his supply chain. She spent days gathering intel, using her connections to piece together his operations. Every detail mattered, and she didn't leave anything to chance.

One night, as she and Slim went over the final details, Theresa felt a mix of excitement and fear. This was it. Her chance to reclaim her throne and exact her revenge.

"We move tomorrow," she said, her voice steady. "We hit his main warehouse, take out his stash, and send a message. No more games."

Slim nodded, his eyes filled with determination. "We got your back, Sugar. Let's do this."

The night was dark, the air heavy with anticipation. Theresa and her crew moved through the shadows, their footsteps silent as they approached Big D's warehouse. The building loomed ahead, guarded by armed men who had no idea what was coming.

Theresa signaled to her team, and they sprang into action. The first guards went down quietly, their bodies dragged into the darkness. The crew moved swiftly, each step bringing them closer to their target.

Inside, the warehouse was a maze of crates and containers, filled with drugs and money. Theresa's heart pounded as they moved through the space, planting explosives and marking targets.

As they reached the center of the warehouse, Theresa spotted Big D's right-hand man, Rico, overseeing the operation. She motioned to Slim, and they moved in, guns drawn.

"Rico," Theresa called out, her voice echoing through the space. "Time's up."

Rico spun around, his eyes widening as he saw her. "Sugar? What the hell—"

Theresa didn't give him a chance to finish. She fired, the shot ringing out in the stillness. Rico fell, clutching his chest, his eyes filled with shock.

"Let's go," Theresa shouted, her crew moving quickly to finish the job. The explosives were set, the warehouse rigged to blow. They had minutes to get out before the whole place went up in flames.

They moved fast, exiting the building just as the first explosion rocked the air. Theresa looked back, watching as the warehouse was consumed by fire, a symbol of her revenge. But she knew this was just the beginning. Big D wouldn't go down without a fight.

The next few days were a whirlwind of retaliation and counterattacks. Big D struck back hard, his men hitting Theresa's territory, trying to regain control. The streets were a war zone, each side pushing the other to the brink.

Theresa's determination never wavered. She fought back with everything she had, using her wits and her allies to stay one step ahead. She knew the risks, knew that every move could be her last, but she was driven by a fierce need for vengeance.

One night, as she was catching her breath in a safe house, Keisha walked in, her face grim. "Sugar, we got a problem. Big D's planning something big. We need to hit him first."

Theresa nodded, her mind racing. "What's his next move?"

Keisha handed her a piece of paper. "He's meeting with his suppliers tomorrow night. If we take them out, we cripple his operation."

Theresa studied the information, her heart pounding with anticipation. "This is it. We take him down, once and for all."

The following night, Theresa and her crew moved through the city, their destination clear. They reached the meeting spot, a secluded warehouse on the edge of town. The air was tense, every shadow a potential threat.

Theresa signaled to her team, and they moved in, surrounding the building. She took a deep breath, her finger on the trigger, ready for whatever came next.

As they burst through the doors, chaos erupted. Big D's men scrambled, reaching for their weapons, but Theresa's crew was faster. The gunfire was deafening, the air filled with smoke and screams.

Theresa spotted Big D in the center of the chaos, his eyes wide with shock. She moved towards him, her gun aimed steady. "This ends now, D."

Big D sneered, raising his own weapon. "You think you can take me down, Sugar? You ain't got what it takes."

Theresa fired, the shot ringing out loud and clear. Big D fell, his body hitting the ground with a thud. The room fell silent, the battle over.

Theresa stood over him, her heart racing. She had done it. She had taken down Big D. But the cost was high, the battle far from over. She knew there were still challenges ahead, still enemies waiting in the shadows.

As she walked out of the warehouse, the night air cool against her skin, Theresa felt a sense of relief and determination. The game was far from over, but she was ready for whatever came next.

The night was dark, the future uncertain. But Theresa was ready for the battles ahead. She had faced the darkness and come out stronger. The stakes were higher than ever, but so were the rewards. And Theresa was willing to gamble it all.

As the city buzzed with the news of Big D's downfall, Theresa knew one thing for sure: the fight was far from over. She was ready for the battles ahead, ready to face whatever came her way. The streets were unforgiving, but so was she. And as long as she had her allies by her side, she knew they could take on the world.

The game was dangerous, but Theresa was a player, and she wasn't going to let anyone stand in her way. The struggle was real, but so was her determination. The game was on, and she was in it to win it.

Chapter 14: The Final Play

Theresa moved through the darkened streets with a sense of purpose, her mind focused on the final showdown with Big D. She had assembled a loyal crew, each member ready to risk everything to bring down their common enemy. The tension in the air was palpable, every shadow a potential threat, every noise a possible ambush.

She gathered her team in an abandoned warehouse, the dim light casting eerie shadows on the walls. Slim, Keisha, and a handful of their most trusted allies stood around a makeshift table, studying the plans she had laid out.

"This is it," Theresa said, her voice steady but filled with determination. "Tonight, we end this. We hit Big D hard and take him out for good."

Slim nodded, his eyes reflecting the same resolve. "We're with you, Sugar. Whatever it takes."

Theresa's gaze swept over her crew, each face etched with grim determination. They knew the risks, understood the stakes. There was no turning back now.

The plan was set in motion with military precision. Theresa's crew moved through the city, slipping past Big D's patrols and setting up their positions. They had eyes on the warehouse where Big D was holed up, waiting for the perfect moment to strike.

As they approached the warehouse, Theresa's heart pounded in her chest. She could feel the tension, the anticipation of what was to come. She signaled to her team, and they moved in, silent and deadly.

But just as they were about to breach the doors, a sudden shout rang out. "It's a trap!"

Theresa spun around, her gun drawn, just in time to see one of her own men, Marcus, pointing a gun at her. Betrayal flashed in his eyes.

"Sorry, Sugar," Marcus sneered. "Big D made me a better offer."

Theresa's blood boiled. "You traitorous son of a bitch!"

Before Marcus could pull the trigger, Slim tackled him, the two men struggling on the ground. The air was filled with shouts and gunfire as Big D's men swarmed out of the warehouse, their weapons blazing.

Theresa ducked behind a crate, her mind racing. The betrayal had thrown their plans into chaos, but she couldn't let it end here. She returned fire, taking down two of Big D's men, her eyes searching for Slim.

The battle was fierce, each side fighting with everything they had. Theresa's crew was outnumbered, but they fought with a ferocity born of desperation and determination. She saw Keisha take down one of Big D's lieutenants, her face set in grim resolve.

But the tide was turning. Big D's men were closing in, their sheer numbers overwhelming. Theresa knew they needed a miracle to survive this.

In the midst of the chaos, she spotted Big D himself, standing at the edge of the battlefield, a smug smile on his face. Rage surged through her veins. This was the moment she had been waiting for.

Theresa charged forward, her gun blazing, cutting a path through the chaos. Big D saw her coming, his smile fading as he raised his own weapon. The two of them locked eyes, the world around them fading into a blur.

"Come on, Sugar," Big D taunted. "Show me what you got."

Theresa didn't hesitate. She fired, the bullets tearing through the air. Big D ducked, returning fire, the shots whizzing past her head. They circled each other, each one looking for an opening, a weakness.

The fight was brutal, each shot echoing with years of rivalry and hatred. Theresa felt a bullet graze her arm, the pain sharp but ignorable. She gritted her teeth, pushing through the pain, her eyes never leaving Big D.

"You think you can take me down?" Big D snarled, his voice filled with venom. "You ain't got what it takes, Sugar."

Theresa's face twisted with fury. "Watch me."

She lunged forward, her gun firing. The bullets found their mark, hitting Big D in the chest. He staggered, his eyes wide with shock, before falling to the ground, blood pooling around him.

Theresa stood over him, her chest heaving with exertion and adrenaline. "It's over, D. You're done."

Big D coughed, blood staining his lips. "You think this changes anything? There's always someone else... someone stronger..."

Theresa shook her head, her voice cold. "Not this time."

As Big D's body went still, the remaining fight drained out of his men. They dropped their weapons, surrendering to the inevitable. Theresa's crew moved in, securing the area, their faces showing a mixture of relief and exhaustion.

Slim approached Theresa, his face bruised but smiling. "We did it, Sugar. It's over."

Theresa nodded, her body trembling with the aftermath of battle. "Yeah. We did it."

But as she looked around at the carnage, the cost of their victory hit her. Friends lost, blood spilled, all for control of these unforgiving streets. She knew the fight for power would never truly end, but for now, they had won.

The night was dark, but for the first time in a long while, Theresa felt a glimmer of hope. She had taken down her greatest enemy, but the challenges ahead were still daunting. She had to rebuild, to solidify her control, and to ensure the safety of her crew and her territory.

As the first light of dawn began to break, Theresa stood with Slim and Keisha, looking out over the city. The future was uncertain, but they had proven their strength, their resolve.

"We keep moving forward," Theresa said, her voice steady. "We rebuild. We protect what's ours."

Slim nodded, his eyes filled with determination. "We got your back, Sugar. Always."

Keisha smiled, her face showing a mixture of pride and determination. "Together, we're unstoppable."

The game was far from over, but Theresa was ready for whatever came next. She had faced betrayal, violence, and the darkest parts of the streets, and she had come out stronger. The stakes were higher than ever, but so were the rewards. And Theresa was willing to gamble it all.

As the city began to wake, the echoes of the night's battle still lingering in the air, Theresa knew one thing for sure: she was a player in this dangerous game, and she wasn't going to let anyone stand in her way. The struggle was real, but so was her determination. The game was on, and she was in it to win it.

Chapter 15: Aftermath

The sun rose over the city, casting a harsh light on the aftermath of the battle. Theresa sat on the steps of the warehouse, her body aching from the fight, her mind a whirlwind of thoughts. The physical toll of the final showdown with Big D was evident in every bruise, every cut, every ounce of fatigue that weighed her down. But it was the emotional toll that hit her hardest.

The streets were littered with the remnants of their clash, the air still thick with the scent of gunpowder and blood. Theresa watched as her crew moved through the wreckage, their faces etched with exhaustion and grief. They had won, but at what cost? Friends had been lost, lives shattered, all for control of this unforgiving urban jungle.

Slim walked over, his own face marked with the signs of battle. He sat down beside her, his silence speaking volumes. After a moment, he finally spoke, his voice rough. "We did it, Sugar. But damn, it took a lot out of us."

Theresa nodded, her gaze distant. "Yeah. We paid a heavy price. But we had to do it. There was no other way."

As the day wore on, Theresa couldn't shake the weight of her choices. She had fought so hard to climb to the top, to survive in a world that was constantly trying to pull her down. But now, sitting amidst the wreckage of her victory, she couldn't help but reflect on the path that had led her here.

She thought back to her early days, hustling on Backpage just to make ends meet. The streets had taught her to be tough, to be ruthless. She had learned to navigate the dangers, to use her beauty and brains to get ahead. But every step she had taken had come with a price, every victory tinged with loss.

Theresa closed her eyes, the memories flooding back. The betrayal of Marcus, the constant threat of Big D, the fear of losing everything she had built. She had faced it all, fought through it all, but the scars remained. Each one a reminder of the sacrifices she had made.

Keisha joined them, her face drawn with fatigue. "You okay, T?"

Theresa looked up, forcing a smile. "I'm alright. Just...thinking."

Keisha nodded, her eyes understanding. "We've been through hell. But we're still standing."

That evening, Theresa stood on the balcony of her apartment, looking out over the city. The lights twinkled below, each one a symbol of the life she had fought so hard to claim. She knew she had to start rebuilding, to solidify her control and protect her territory. But first, she needed to make peace with her decisions.

Slim found her there, his presence a comforting weight. "What's on your mind, Sugar?"

Theresa sighed, her gaze still fixed on the skyline. "Just...everything. The choices I made, the people we lost. It's a lot to take in."

Slim nodded, his hand resting on her shoulder. "We did what we had to do. We survived. And now, we rebuild."

Theresa turned to him, her eyes filled with determination. "You're right. We rebuild. We protect what's ours."

The days that followed were a blur of activity. Theresa and her crew worked tirelessly to fortify their territory, to regain control and ensure their safety. They patched up wounds, both physical and emotional, and began the process of moving forward.

But the scars remained. Every corner of the city held memories of battles fought and lives lost. Theresa carried those memories with her, a constant reminder of the cost of power.

One night, as she sat in her office, Keisha walked in, holding a bottle of whiskey. "Thought you might need this."

Theresa smiled, taking the bottle. "Thanks, K."

They sat in silence for a while, the weight of their shared experiences hanging between them. Finally, Keisha spoke, her voice soft. "You ever wonder if it was all worth it?"

Theresa took a long sip, her eyes distant. "Every day. But we didn't have a choice. The streets don't give you options. You take what you can, or you get taken."

Keisha nodded, her expression thoughtful. "I guess that's the truth. But still, it's hard."

Theresa reached out, squeezing Keisha's hand. "We made it through. And we're stronger for it. But yeah, it's hard. Real hard."

As the weeks passed, Theresa found a strange sense of closure settling over her. She had fought her battles, faced her demons, and come out the other side. The scars were there, but they were a part of her story, a testament to her strength and resilience.

One evening, as she stood on the balcony once more, Slim joined her, his arm around her shoulders. "We did good, Sugar. Real good."

Theresa leaned into him, a small smile playing on her lips. "Yeah, we did. But there's still work to be done."

Slim nodded, his eyes filled with determination. "Always. But we got this."

The night was dark, the city alive with possibilities. Theresa had faced the darkest parts of the streets and survived. She had made peace with her choices, but the fight was far from over. The stakes were higher than ever, but so were the rewards. And Theresa was willing to gamble it all.

As the city buzzed with the echoes of their victory, Theresa knew one thing for sure: the game was far from over. She was ready for the battles ahead, ready to face whatever came her way. The streets were unforgiving, but so was she. And as long as she had her allies by her side, she knew they could take on the world.

The game was dangerous, but Theresa was a player, and she wasn't going to let anyone stand in her way. The struggle was real, but so was her determination. The game was on, and she was in it to win it.

Chapter 16: Mia's Tragedy

Theresa walked through the streets, her eyes scanning the familiar faces and corners she knew so well. The city was a jungle, and she had learned to navigate it with a fierce determination. But as she turned the corner, she saw a face that stopped her in her tracks.

Mia was a young girl, barely out of her teens, with a look in her eyes that Theresa recognized all too well. She was standing on the corner, dressed to catch attention, her eyes darting nervously as she scanned the streets. Theresa's heart ached as she saw a reflection of her younger self in the girl.

Theresa approached her slowly, her voice gentle. "Hey there, you new around here?"

Mia looked up, startled, but then relaxed when she saw Theresa's friendly expression. "Yeah, just tryin' to make some money. You know how it is."

Theresa nodded, her heart heavy. "Yeah, I know. What's your name?"

"Mia," the girl replied, a hint of defiance in her voice.

"Well, Mia, I'm Sugar. And I'm tellin' you now, this life ain't what you think it is. It's dangerous. You need to be careful."

Mia shrugged, her eyes flashing with determination. "I can handle myself. I need the money. Got no other choice."

Theresa sighed, seeing so much of her younger self in the girl's bravado. "Listen, I've been where you are. It's tough, but there are other ways. You don't have to do this."

But Mia;s mind was made up. She had been drawn into the same cycle that had ensnared so many before her. Theresa tried to reach her, to offer her a way out, but the pull of the streets was strong.

Despite Theresa's warnings, Mia continued to work the corners, getting deeper into the life. Theresa watched from a distance, her heart breaking as she saw the girl making the same mistakes she had made years ago.

One evening, as Theresa was making her rounds, she spotted Mia talking to a rough-looking man. The exchange looked tense, and Theresa's instincts screamed danger. She moved closer, trying to listen in.

"Look, I told you I'd have the money!" Mia was saying, her voice shaky.

The man grabbed her arm, his face twisted with anger. "You better, or there's gonna be trouble."

Theresa stepped in, her voice cold and authoritative. "Let her go. Now."

The man looked at Theresa, recognizing her. He released Mia and backed off, muttering under his breath. Theresa watched him go, then turned to Mia.

"You okay?" she asked, her voice softening.

Mia nodded, tears brimming in her eyes. "Yeah, thanks."

Theresa sighed, wishing she could do more. "Mia, you gotta get out of this life. It's gonna chew you up and spit you out."

Mia wiped her eyes, her face hardening. "I can't. I need the money. I got people dependin' on me."

Theresa understood all too well, but she also knew the cost. "Just be careful, okay? And if you need help, come find me."

The weeks passed, and Mia's situation grew more desperate. She was getting deeper into debt with dangerous people, and the toll was starting to show. Theresa tried to help, offering money and advice, but Mia's pride and circumstances kept her trapped.

One night, the inevitable happened. Theresa received a call from Keisha, her voice filled with urgency. "Sugar, it's Mia. She's in trouble."

Theresa's heart raced as she hurried to the address Keisha gave her. She found Mia in a dark alley, badly beaten and barely conscious. Her attackers were long gone, leaving her broken and bleeding on the cold pavement.

Theresa knelt beside her, her hands trembling. "Mia, can you hear me? It's Sugar."

Mia's eyes fluttered open, tears streaming down her face. "I'm sorry... I should've listened..."

Theresa's heart shattered as she cradled the girl in her arms. "It's okay, Mia. I'm here. I'm gonna get you help."

But it was too late. Mia's injuries were too severe, and she slipped away before the ambulance could arrive. Theresa sat there, holding her, tears streaming down her face, cursing the brutal cycle that had claimed yet another life.

Mia's death hit Theresa hard. She had tried so hard to save her, to break the cycle, but the streets had claimed another victim. The weight of it pressed down on her, a stark reminder of the harsh reality of the life she had fought so hard to escape.

Theresa stood at Mia's makeshift memorial, a collection of candles and flowers left by those who had known her. She felt a deep sense of failure and grief, but also a renewed determination. She couldn't save Mia, but she could fight to make sure no one else suffered the same fate.

Keisha joined her, her face etched with sorrow. "You did everything you could, T. Sometimes, the streets just take and take."

Theresa nodded, her eyes burning with unshed tears. "I know. But we gotta keep fightin'. For Mia, and for all the others like her."

Slim approached, placing a hand on Theresa's shoulder. "We're with you, Sugar. Always."

As the night fell, Theresa stood with her crew, looking out over the city. The battle was far from over, but she was ready. She had faced loss and tragedy, but her resolve was stronger than ever. The stakes were higher, the fight more brutal, but she was determined to keep going.

The game was dangerous, but Theresa was a player, and she wasn't going to let anyone stand in her way. The struggle was real, but so was her determination. The game was on, and she was in it to win it.

As the candles flickered in the darkness, Theresa made a silent vow. She would fight for those who couldn't fight for themselves. She would honor Mia's memory by continuing the battle. The streets were unforgiving, but so was she. And as long as she had her allies by her side, she knew they could take on the world.

Chapter 17: Final Confrontation

Theresa sat in her apartment, staring out the window at the city she had fought so hard to control. The streets were quiet now, the aftermath of the recent chaos still hanging in the air. She had faced down her enemies, survived betrayal, and navigated the brutal realities of street life. But now, it was time to confront the demons that haunted her and make peace with her past.

She picked up a photo from the table beside her—a picture of herself as a young girl, full of dreams and innocence. The girl in the photo had no idea what lay ahead, the battles she would face, the scars she would carry. Theresa felt a pang of sadness but also a sense of resolve. She had come too far to let her past dictate her future.

Theresa met with Jai and Rose in a small café, a rare moment of normalcy in their chaotic lives. Jai, who had once been her rival and then her closest ally, and Rose, the seasoned veteran who had seen it all, sat across from her. They had been through hell together, and now it was time to plan for a different kind of future.

"Y'all, we need to talk," Theresa began, her voice steady but serious. "We've been through a lot. But I'm thinkin' it's time to leave this life behind."

Jai looked up, surprise and curiosity in her eyes. "You serious, T? After all we've built?"

Theresa nodded. "Yeah, I'm serious. I'm tired of the blood, the violence. I want something different. I want a future where we don't have to look over our shoulders every damn day."

Rose, her face lined with years of hard living, leaned forward. "What you got in mind, Sugar? We can't just walk away. People don't forget."

Theresa sighed, her mind racing with plans and possibilities. "I know it ain't gonna be easy. But I'm thinkin' we start fresh. Somewhere new, away from all this. We got the money. We just need to make the move."

The conversation was intense, each of them weighing the risks and rewards. They had built their lives on the streets, but the cost had been high. Now, the prospect of something different, something better, was both terrifying and exhilarating.

As they talked, a new resolve took hold. They had faced down their enemies, survived the worst the streets had to offer. If they could do that, they could rebuild their lives somewhere new.

"We gotta plan it right," Jai said, her voice firm. "We can't just up and leave. We need to cover our tracks, make sure no one follows us."

Theresa nodded. "Agreed. We'll take it step by step. But first, we need to tie up loose ends here."

—-

The next few days were a whirlwind of activity. Theresa and her crew moved quickly, settling old debts, making arrangements, and preparing for their departure. It was dangerous work, but they were determined.

Theresa also took time to reflect on her journey. She visited the places that had shaped her—the rundown apartment where she had grown up, the corners where she had hustled, the clubs where she had made her name. Each place held memories, both good and bad, and she faced them all with a sense of closure.

One evening, she stood at the edge of the city, looking out over the skyline. The city had been her battlefield, her prison, and her home. But now, it was time to say goodbye. She felt a sense of peace wash over her, knowing she had done everything she could to survive and thrive in this unforgiving world.

Theresa gathered with Jai and Rose one last time before they made their move. The plan was set, and they were ready to start a new chapter in their lives.

"You sure about this, T?" Rose asked, her voice tinged with worry.

Theresa smiled, a genuine smile that reached her eyes. "Yeah, Rose. I'm sure. We've earned this. It's time for something better."

Jai nodded, her expression one of determination. "We got each other. That's all we need."

The night of their departure was tense, each of them on high alert as they made their way to the rendezvous point. They moved through the city with practiced ease, their eyes and ears attuned to every sound, every shadow.

As they reached the edge of the city, a car waiting to take them to their new life, Theresa took one last look back. The city that had been her battleground was behind her now. Ahead lay the promise of a new beginning.

They climbed into the car, the engine starting with a low rumble. As they drove away, the tension began to ease, replaced by a sense of hope and excitement.

Theresa sat back, a small smile playing on her lips. She had faced her past, made peace with her decisions, and now she was ready for the future. The road ahead was uncertain, but she was ready for whatever came next.

The night was dark, but the future was bright with possibilities. Theresa had faced the darkest parts of the streets and come out stronger. She had made peace with her past, but the fight was far from over. The stakes were higher than ever, but so were the rewards. And Theresa was willing to gamble it all.

As the city faded into the distance, Theresa knew one thing for sure: the game was far from over. She was ready for the battles ahead, ready to face whatever came her way. The streets were unforgiving, but so was she. And as long as she had her allies by her side, she knew they could take on the world.

The game was dangerous, but Theresa was a player, and she wasn't going to let anyone stand in her way. The struggle was real, but so was her determination. The game was on, and she was in it to win it.

Chapter 18: Sad Closure

Theresa stood at the edge of Mia's makeshift memorial, the flickering candles casting ghostly shadows on the pavement. Mia's death weighed heavily on her heart, a stark reminder of the brutal cycle of the streets they had all been trapped in. The loss of the young girl, so full of promise and potential, was a somber testament to the life Theresa, Jai, and Rose were determined to leave behind.

Theresa's eyes glistened with unshed tears as she placed a single white rose among the other flowers. Jai stood beside her, silent but supportive, while Rose hung back, her weathered face etched with a mix of sorrow and resolve.

Mia had been so much like Theresa in her younger days—headstrong, desperate, and unyielding. Seeing her fall victim to the same life that had once threatened to consume her own ignited a deep, painful anger within Theresa. She had tried to warn Mia, to save her, but the streets had their own cruel ways.

"This ain't right, T," Jai murmured, her voice choked with emotion. "She didn't deserve this."

Theresa nodded, her throat tight. "None of us did, Jai. But this is the life we were dealt. We just gotta make sure it ends with us."

—-

The trio spent the next few days preparing to leave the city. They knew they couldn't escape their past entirely, but they could carve out a new future, one that wasn't tainted by the constant threat of violence and betrayal. The decision to move was bittersweet; they were leaving behind everything they had known, but they were also shedding the chains of their former lives.

Theresa, Jai, and Rose gathered one last time at Mia's memorial. The sun was setting, casting a warm, golden glow over the city. It was a beautiful, yet melancholic scene, reflecting the duality of their emotions.

Theresa took a deep breath, her voice trembling as she spoke. "Mia didn't make it, but we will. We owe it to her to live better, to be better."

Rose stepped forward, her eyes filled with a rare vulnerability. "I've seen too many girls like Mia go down this path. We gotta honor her by breakin' the cycle. No more livin' like this."

Jai nodded, tears streaming down her face. "We're gonna do it, T. For Mia, and for ourselves."

—-

The next morning, they packed their belongings and prepared to leave the city for good. The air was heavy with unspoken words and unexpressed fears, but there was also a sense of hopeful anticipation. They were stepping into the unknown, but they were doing it together.

As they drove away, the city skyline gradually faded into the distance. Theresa glanced back one last time, her heart a mix of sorrow and relief. She knew she was leaving behind a part of herself, but she was also embracing a new beginning.

The journey was long, but it gave them time to reflect on their past and plan for their future. They talked about their dreams, their fears, and their hopes for a life free from the shackles of the streets.

"We ain't just survivors, we're warriors," Jai said, her voice strong with conviction. "We fought hard to get here, and we ain't never goin' back."

Theresa smiled, her heart swelling with pride. "Damn right. We're gonna build somethin' new, somethin' better."

—-

When they finally arrived at their new home, a small town far removed from the chaos of the city, it felt like a weight had been lifted from their shoulders. The air was cleaner, the streets quieter, and for the first time in a long time, they felt a sense of peace.

They spent the first few days settling in, getting to know their neighbors, and starting to build their new lives. It wasn't easy—there were moments of doubt and fear, but they supported each other through it all.

Theresa found herself reflecting often on Mia's legacy. The young girl's death had been a catalyst for their change, a painful reminder of why they had to leave the streets behind. Mia's memory spurred them on, fueling their determination to create a better future.

One evening, as they sat on the porch of their new home, the sun setting in a blaze of colors, Theresa turned to Jai and Rose. "We made it out. We're gonna make this work."

Rose nodded, a rare smile on her face. "We got each other. That's more than enough."

Jai raised her glass, her eyes shining with hope. "To Mia. And to us."

They clinked their glasses, a silent promise passing between them. They had faced their past, mourned their losses, and now, they were ready to embrace the future.

The night was calm, the future stretching out before them like a blank canvas. Theresa had faced the darkest parts of the streets and come out stronger. She had made peace with her past, and now she was ready to move forward.

As the stars twinkled overhead, Theresa knew one thing for sure: the struggle had been real, but so was their victory. They had survived, and now they were ready to thrive. The streets had taught them to be tough, but now they were free to be themselves.

The game was over, but life was just beginning. And Theresa was ready to make the most of it. With Jai and Rose by her side, she knew they could face anything. They had each other, and that was all they needed.

Don't miss out!

Visit the website below and you can sign up to receive emails whenever Rachael Reed publishes a new book. There's no charge and no obligation.

https://books2read.com/r/B-A-WXARB-QUWUD

BOOKS 2 READ

Connecting independent readers to independent writers.

Did you love *Backpage Hustle*? Then you should read *Cartel Bloodline*[1] by Rachael Reed!

[2]

Cartel Bloodline: A Tale of Love, Betrayal, and Survival in the Miami Underworld

In the ruthless streets of Miami, where the Cartel controls eighty percent of the cocaine flowing through the port, power is everything, and trust is a luxury no one can afford. When the most feared gangster, Antonio Brown, falls, he leaves behind a legacy that's more explosive than anyone could've imagined. His death unearths a hidden secret—an illegitimate son, Antonio Lewis, who's about to step into a world where loyalty is bought with blood and betrayal lurks around every corner.

Antonio Lewis, raised far from the chaos of Miami's underworld, gets pulled into the Cartel's deadly embrace when he learns of his father's

---

1. https://books2read.com/u/4jpKMk

2. https://books2read.com/u/4jpKMk

empire. Thrown into a cutthroat game where every ally is a potential enemy, Antonio must navigate the treacherous waters of his father's legacy, battling for his place in the empire while uncovering the dark secrets that threaten to consume him.

Lea, a deadly beauty with a heart of steel, leads The Get Money Girls, a crew of contract killers who live by their own rules. When her cousin falls in a botched hit on the Cartel, Lea vows revenge, unaware that her heart would soon become entangled with the enemy. Antonio and Lea's worlds collide in a storm of passion and deceit, their forbidden love a ticking time bomb ready to explode.

As alliances crumble and enemies close in, Antonio and Lea must face the ultimate betrayal from within their ranks. The lines between love and loyalty blur, and survival becomes a deadly game of cat and mouse. The streets of Miami become a battlefield, where every decision could mean life or death, and the only way out is to fight until the last breath.

Will Antonio rise to claim his father's throne, or will the legacy of the Cartel drag him down into the abyss? Can Lea reconcile her thirst for vengeance with the love that binds her to Antonio, or will the secrets they uncover tear them apart forever?

Cartel Bloodline is a gritty, suspense-filled journey through the dark underbelly of Miami, where power is fleeting, love is dangerous, and the ultimate betrayal could come from the person you trust the most. In this world, nothing is as it seems, and the streets never forget.

Also by Rachael Reed

Codefendant
Codefendant
Once a Cheater
Once a Cheater
Passport Bro
What Happens in Prison
Preference
Sprinkle Sprinkle
Championship Bad
Street Exodus
Street Exodus
Street Royalty
Pawns of Power
SIS
Cartel Bloodline
Get Money Girls
Skip the Games
Til Death Do Us Part
Backpage Hustle